Tough to Tackle

by Matt Christopher

illustrated by Harvey Kidder

SCHOLASTIC INC.
New York Toronto London Auckland Sydney

ISBN 0-590-46384-5

12   4 5 6 7 8 9/0

Printed in the U.S.A.   40

First Scholastic printing, October 1992

For Ernie, Judy and Ginger

Tough to Tackle

1

BOOTS RAYMOND stood on the porch, the September wind whipping his unzipped jacket and toying with his hair. He was thinking.

"Well, are you going to stand there all day or are you coming?" asked Bud Davis, one of the two boys looking up at him from the sidewalk.

Boots flashed a grin, shrugged, and rattled down the steps. He wrapped an arm around Bud's head and gave him a gentle poke in the ribs.

"I was thinking," he said.

Duck Farrell sniffed the air and nodded. "Yep, you were," he agreed. "I smell rubber."

Boots's fist lashed out and Duck dodged it. He lost his balance and fell on his bottom, a look of pain coming over his freckled face.

"You nut," said Boots. "I was only faking. I wasn't going to hit you."

Boots grabbed the redhead's arm and helped him to his feet.

The look of pain disappeared as Duck smiled. "Oh, thank you," he said in a singsong voice.

Boots picked up Duck's blue hat and plopped it on the patch of unruly red hair.

"You okay?" he asked.

"I'm okay," said Duck, dusting off his pants. "But you sure have a funny way of faking."

4

Boots was four inches taller than Duck and twenty pounds heavier, although both were the same age. He had been thinking about playing quarterback on the Apollos football team. He had played quarterback last year on a pickup team and had discovered that he could throw forward passes a mile and carry the ball almost every time with a good, substantial gain. He was a *natural* quarterback.

"What position you guys shooting for?" he asked.

"Quarterback," said Bud.

"Halfback," answered Duck, straightening his hat. "What position *you* shooting for? Guard?"

"Guard, my eye. I'm shooting for quarterback, too."

"Quarterback?" Duck stared, then looked at Bud. Bud was a year older than the boys, but he was Duck's size. Boots had seen Bud play quarterback. Bud was good. But Boots, being bigger, was sure that he could gain yardage better than Bud.

"Yes, quarterback," Boots said. "That's where the action is. Who hasn't heard of Roman Gabriel, Joe Namath and Len Dawson?"

"Okay, who hasn't? They're quarterbacks on professional teams."

"See that? Everybody knows who they are. But name one guard."

Duck's forehead knitted.

"You can't," said Boots promptly. "That goes to show you. It's a quarterback people remember. Not a guard. Not a tackle."

"Gene Hickerson! Jim Kanicki! Alan Page!" Duck cried out the names in rapid order.

Boots blinked. Leave it to Duck, he thought. He probably could name every player in the NFL and the AFL.

"But you had to have time to think about it," he said. "Quarterbacks' names pop into your head like one, two, three."

"That's only because you're interested in quarterbacks instead of guards and tackles," replied Duck. "Without guards and tackles, what good is a quarterback?"

"No good."

"So what are you arguing about?"

"Come on," Bud interrupted. "Let's go or we won't be playing *any* position!"

They headed for the field.

Boots was glad football season had come around. His sister Gail wasn't enough to fill the gap that their brother Tom had left. Tom and he used to wrestle. Tom was bigger and had pinned Boots as often as Boots had pinned him. Boots knew Tom would let him win just so he wouldn't get discouraged and not wrestle anymore. But it was fun just the same.

They had also played basketball and pitch and catch. Boots had hoped that all the exercise would keep him from gaining too much weight. He was pretty big as it was.

Then Tom had enlisted in the Marines and was sent overseas to Vietnam. That was only a few months ago, but it seemed like years to Boots.

When they reached the football field, at least twenty guys were already there. They were throwing and catching footballs and making more noise than a jungle full of animals. No one was in uniform. Coach Bo Higgins had promised he'd pass them out after today's workout.

Boots saw the coach with another man on a bench in front of the third-base bleachers. The field was used for baseball in summer. In another week or so it would be marked with white lines every five yards and the goal posts would be put up.

"There's a hefty man for us, Bo," said the man sitting with the coach. "Hi, son! What's your name?"

"Boots Raymond," said Boots shyly. He shrugged. "It's Theodore, but everybody calls me Boots."

Bo Higgins smiled. He was tall and broad-shouldered, and wore a red baseball cap. "Hi, Boots," he greeted. "This is Coach Dekay. He's my assistant this year."

Mr. Dekay was still smiling. He was

taller than Bo, but thinner around the shoulders. "A few more boys like you, Boots, and we'd have a real strong line."

Boots's jaw dropped. "Do I have to play on the line?" he asked disappointedly. "Can't I play in the backfield? Like . . . quarterback?"

Mr. Dekay chuckled and exchanged a look with Coach Higgins.

Bo met Boots's eyes squarely. "What do you weigh, Boots?"

"A hundred and thirty-nine pounds."

Bo Higgins shook his head. "Sorry, Boots. A hundred and twenty-five is the limit for backfield players, and a hundred and forty for linemen. We have to have that ruling, otherwise a heavy boy like yourself wouldn't have much trouble tearing through a line that could be made up of players pretty light in weight. Didn't you read the form your parents signed?"

The coach's reply struck Boots like a bell of doom.

"I — I guess I didn't," he said dismally.

2

"ONE . . . TWO! One . . . two! Spread those legs, Boots! Raise those elbows, Vic! One . . . two! One . . . two!"

Coach Bo Higgins was leading the team in calisthenics, jumping with his legs spread apart and his arms straight up in graceful form.

"Down on your backs! Hands behind your heads and your feet together! Now . . . without bending your knees, lift your legs a foot off the ground and hold them there!"

Boots grunted and groaned as he felt the ache come to his legs. He kept his lips pressed tightly and strained to hold up his limbs until the coach gave the word to drop them.

"Okay! Down! Rest a minute!"

The minute seemed the shortest in history.

"Everybody on his feet for the Dead Body drill! All right! Down on your bellies! Side by side with about two feet between you and the next man! Eddie Baker, you're first in line! Get up, jump over each body, and fall flat after you reach the last one! Leo Conway, you're next in line! Follow Eddie! Get the idea?"

"Got it," several guys answered in unison.

After each boy went through the routine at least twice, Coach Higgins let them play catch with footballs for a while. Then he called the boys together and handed each of them a football uniform. The jerseys were red and the pants blue, with the team's name, APOLLOS, on the front of the jerseys. On the backs were the numbers. Boots's was 77.

Coach Higgins knew all the time that he was going to play me on the line, Boots reflected discouragingly. But what position? I suppose I'll have to wait till next practice to find out.

The Apollos had calisthenics the next day and the next. On the third day the coach showed some mercy: He cut the calisthenics time in half. Practice wasn't over, though. Bo Higgins read off a list of names from a clipboard and after each name a position. Boots's name was right on top of the list. And his position: right tackle.

The next players named were:

Richie Powell   *right guard*
Pete Ellis   *right end*
Ralph Patone   *center*
Vic Walker   *left tackle*
Neil Dekay   *left guard*
Eddie Baker   *left end*
Leo Conway   *fullback*
Jackie Preston   *right halfback*
Duck Farrell   *left halfback*
Bud Davis   *quarterback*

"That's the offensive team," said the coach. "Most of the guys will play defensive, too. We're not loaded with enough players to have fresh units go in each time the football changes hands. Leo, you'll play fullback on offense and middle linebacker on defense, for example. Don't worry. We have enough subs so that no one will get so tired he can't walk. Neither Coach Dekay nor I will be that cruel with you."

A chuckle rippled from some of the boys.

"But we want a good team," the coach went on emphatically. "We want players who want to play. If any of you think you're here just to get out of doing chores at home you might as well quit right now. I don't want to waste time with that kind of player. There are a lot of kids who are anxious to play but won't go out for football because they fear they won't have a chance. So drill this into your heads: Be serious about playing football, or hand in your uniform right now."

Boots felt that the coach was talking directly to him, for he wasn't really sure now whether he could be serious about playing football or not. He wanted to play quarterback. That was the position he was set on. That was the position in which he felt he could put his best effort.

Limiting a quarterback's weight to one hundred and twenty-five pounds was a crazy rule, Boots reflected. That was okay for the other backs because they usually ran with the ball. A quarterback seldom ran with it. A quarterback was boss. He called the plays. He handed the ball off to the backs or threw forward passes.

What did a tackle or guard do? Nothing but ram his shoulders against the guy in front of him, or throw a block on somebody. You didn't need brains to play

tackle or guard. Just broad shoulders.

Well — weight, too.

And guts. Yeah, you really had to have guts. You could get a lot of pounding from the other guy. A helmet and shoulder pads weren't all you needed to be able to take that pounding.

"Well, I'm through with my speech," said Bo Higgins. "Are there any among you who want to throw in the towel now?"

His eyes wandered slowly over the boys. They met Boots's eyes and Boots didn't flinch. He wasn't going to admit to Bo that he didn't have his heart one hundred percent in playing just because he couldn't play quarterback. He couldn't. Not in front of all the guys.

He didn't know what he'd do. Maybe

he'd tell the coach tomorrow. Or the day after.

The coach wasn't giving a guy a chance asking him to decide this very minute.

3

THE APOLLOS had intrasquad scrimmage on Thursday and Friday, and Boots Raymond was with the team both days.

He tried to tell himself that he hadn't made up his mind yet what to do, but he knew that the truth was he didn't have the nerve to tell Coach Bo Higgins he wanted to quit.

The coach wouldn't just stand there and take back the uniform without saying something. "Why?" he'd say. "Why are you quitting?"

"Because I don't want to play tackle," Boots would have to answer. "I want to play quarterback."

If his life depended on it he couldn't see himself looking into the coach's eyes and admitting that.

Coach Higgins worked with the offense and Coach Dekay with the defense. It had taken almost all week for the boys to call Mr. Dekay "Coach." A lot of the boys had known him a long time and had always called him "Mr. Dekay."

Boots played both on the offensive and defensive squads. Opposite him was Tony Alo, who alternated positions with him. Tony was tall and wiry and much stronger than he looked. He bucked with his head and his shoulders, and it took all of Boots's strength to push Tony back, to control him. Once Tony caught him off balance and shoved him back on his rear, at which Tony smiled proudly and said, "Thought you were tough, fat stuff."

The remark rattled Boots. He didn't like to be called "fat stuff," "fatso," or any other name referring to his build. But he laughed it off. He knew as well as Tony did that he could lick Tony any day of the week. He had done it.

Forty-three. Twenty-two. Thirty-four.

Forty-three meant that number four, the right halfback, was carrying the ball through the three hole, the hole between left tackle and left guard. Twenty-two meant that the left halfback was carrying the ball through the two hole, the hole between the center and the right guard. Thirty-four meant that the fullback was carrying the ball through the four hole, the hole between the right tackle and the right guard. Those were only a few of the plays Bo Higgins was teaching the team.

They worked on the plays and it seemed to Boots that most of them were on his side of the line. One of the backs was running either through the hole at his left side or through the hole at his right. Some were pass plays to either the right or left ends, but the blocking and the pushing didn't let up on the line. Boots saw no fun in it at all.

Suddenly he thought of something simple he could do without getting banged up. He could do it only when his side had the ball, but even then he'd save a lot of wear and tear on his body. It seemed so simple and great he wondered why he hadn't thought of it sooner.

The next time his squad got the ball, he faced Tony Alo with fierce determination in his eyes. They stood face to face. Boots had discovered by now that Tony didn't fear him one bit. Most of the time Boots would roll over him like a bulldozer, but Tony would come back strong as ever. Sometimes stronger.

"Down!" barked quarterback Bud Davis. "Set! Hut! Hut! Hut!"

Just as Tony started to charge, Boots fell flat on his stomach and curled his arm up over his face. He felt Tony fall on him, and he smiled against the grass that tickled his chin.

The coach's whistle shrilled and Boots got up. He saw that Duck was lying on the ground two yards behind the line of scrimmage, with Tony Alo's arms around his waist.

"Boots," said Bo, staring at him. "Are you all right?"

"Yes. I'm all right."

"Okay, offense. Huddle."

Quickly the offensive team formed a U-shaped huddle with Coach Higgins and quarterback Bud Davis crouched at the mouth of the U. "Try forty-three," advised the coach. "Know what that one is, Jackie?"

"Yes, sir," replied right halfback Jackie Preston. "I take the handoff from Bud and break through the three hole."

"Right." The coach slapped his hands once hard. "Let's go!"

This time Boots didn't fall on his stomach. He stood on his feet, blocking Tony Alo. Suddenly Tony dodged past him and broke through the line. Boots then turned to block an oncoming linebacker. He stumbled and felt the guy's knees strike him in the ribs.

The whistle blew and Boots saw that Jackie had made a gain of four yards.

"Okay. That's it for today," said the coach.

It was the best announcement Boots had heard all day. Both his shoulders ached, and his ribs where he had been kicked.

"Man, what a stupid position," he said as he and Bud and Duck headed for home and a hot shower. "Every bone in my body aches."

Duck laughed. "Quit complaining. Look what that poor guy playing opposite you went through."

Boots grinned through the sweat drying on his dirt-smudged face. "Yeah," he said, thinking about Tony Alo. "Guess I did shake him up a little."

He'd give it one more day, he thought. One more day and then he'd tell Coach Bo Higgins he was finished. Football wasn't for him.

When he arrived home from school on Friday Mom told him that there was a letter from Tom.

"Read it," she said, her green eyes sparkling as she smiled at him. She was barely an inch taller than he.

I miss my drums. One of my buddies had a transistor radio which we'd listen to, but Charlie shot it out of his hand one day. [Boots had learned from previous letters that Charlie meant the enemy, the Viet Cong.] It gets very lonesome at times. I miss the fights I had with Gail and wrestling with Boots. I suppose by the time I get back home he'll be able to pin me in nothing flat.

I'm happy to hear he went out for football. It's a good contact sport and should prepare him in many ways for the future.

What position is he playing? Tell him to drop me a letter and tell me all about it. I was a flanker for good old Warren High. Remember? Pray for me, everybody.

Love,
Tom

4

BOOTS RAYMOND didn't know what to do. He had planned to hand in his uniform right after practice tonight and tell Coach Bo Higgins that he was through.

But the letter from Tom changed things. He folded it and clumsily put it back into the envelope.

"Did you write and tell him that I was going out for football?" he asked without looking up.

"No. Your father did. Don't look so

32

glum. Don't you think Tom is pleased to know you've gone out for football?"

"Oh, sure, he is. But . . ."

"But what?"

"Oh — nothing." He turned and started for his room.

"Where are you going, Boots?"

"I'm going to put on my uniform. We're practicing tonight, too."

She looked at him thoughtfully. "Why don't you write to Tom this evening?" she said. "He'd like you to, you know."

"And tell him I'm playing tackle?" snorted Boots. He headed quickly to his room before his mother could say anything more.

He got into his football gear and left the house. Eddie Baker and Leo Conway were already at the field.

"Hi," he greeted them.

"Hi," they said. "Where are Bud and Duck?"

He shrugged. "They'll be coming."

He sat on the grass some ten feet away from them, broke off a stem, and put it between his teeth. Eddie Baker and Leo Conway were snobs. He wished they played on another team. Eddie played a trumpet in the school band and Leo was sports writer for the junior high school paper.

Who can't play a trumpet? You just had to take lessons. And who can't write a sports column? You didn't need a basketful of brains to do that.

Suddenly Boots felt foolish thinking such thoughts about Leo and Eddie. They just had different interests than he had. What was wrong about that?

A car drove up with Coach Dekay behind the wheel. A half-dozen uniformed kids scrambled out of it. A few minutes later Coach Bo Higgins drove up and another half-dozen kids piled out of his car. Bud Davis and Duck Farrell showed up at the same time.

They did calisthenics for ten minutes, then practiced running and pass plays. Bud did most of the passwork. Pete Ellis and Eddie Baker, the ends, did most of the catching. All three were pretty rusty. Bud was either throwing behind the receivers or too far ahead of them. Only about one out of four passes was right on target.

"By baseball season you'll be as good as Lamonica," kidded Boots, laughing.

The sun began to set fast over the hills in the west.

"When's our first game, Coach?" Bud asked when practice was over.

"We'll find out next week when the schedules are handed out," replied Bo Higgins.

Writing a letter was just as hard as writing an essay. But maybe a letter would make Tom feel better. Tom had sounded pretty lonesome and unhappy in his letter.

Dear Tom,
Mom said that Dad told you I went out for football. I wanted to play quarterback but Coach Higgins said I'm too heavy. A backfield man can't weigh over 125 pounds, he said. So he put me on the line. I'm playing right tackle. It's a stupid position. All you do is block on offense and try to bust through the line and get the ball carrier on defense. I'm playing both offense and defense.

I wish they would change the rule about

weights. I think I can play quarterback a lot better than tackle. I'm a poor tackle. I guess lousy is a better word.

Do you think it's okay if I told Coach Higgins that I don't want to play anymore? I sure would like your opinion.

Love,
Boots

5

ON WEDNESDAY evening Coach Higgins handed out two sheets of paper to each player. They contained the schedule and the roster of the Apollos.

Schedule

Sept. 18	Apollos vs. Flyers	School field
	Starbirds vs. Argonauts	Town field
Sept. 25	Apollos vs. Starbirds	School field
	Flyers vs. Argonauts	Town field
Oct. 2	Apollos vs. Argonauts	Town field
	Flyers vs. Starbirds	School field
Oct. 9	Apollos vs. Flyers	Town field
	Starbirds vs. Argonauts	School field

Oct. 16	Apollos vs. Starbirds	Town field
	Flyers vs. Argonauts	School field
Oct. 23	Apollos vs. Argonauts	School field
	Flyers vs. Starbirds	Town field

Roster

Number	Name	Position
77	Boots Raymond	RT
65	Richie Powell	RG
80	Pete Ellis	RE
50	Ralph Patone	C
76	Vic Walker	LT
61	Neil Dekay	LG
84	Eddie Baker	LE
48	Leo Conway	FB, ML*
22	Jackie Preston	RHB, RF*
21	Duck Farrell	LHB, LF*
10	Bud Davis	QB, S*
88	Dale Robin	RE, LE
62	Mike Brink	RG, LG
75	Tony Alo	RT, LT
33	Dick Buckley	RHB, LHB

* ML = middle linebacker.
  RF = right flanker.   LF = left flanker.
  S = safety.

"Wow!" cried Boots. "September eighteenth! That's this Saturday!"

The team worked on running plays and passes. Coach Higgins had to leave early, so Coach Dekay stayed with them the rest of the time. He put them through a tough blocking exercise, concentrating on the guards and tackles.

Boots had thought that Coach Dekay was quite a mild man, but now that Coach Higgins wasn't there the assistant coach showed how tough he really was.

"C'mon, Richie! Hold out your arms! Drive! Drive!"

He didn't show any favoritism. He yelled at almost everyone, including Boots.

"Boots, you're telegraphing your moves! Keep your head steady and your eyes on the man in front of you! And hit with your full body, not just a shoulder!"

Boots tightened his mouth. He realized he had been glancing to the right and left of the man in front of him, looking for the best way to charge through after the ball carrier. Doing that would give his move away, all right. Telegraphing it, as Coach Dekay had put it.

On the next play he didn't move his eyes or his head a single inch. He stood like a statue facing Tony Alo, and from the corners of his eyes he was able to see on either side of him.

The Apollos practiced again on Thursday. Coach Higgins was there but Boots still got chewed out by Coach Dekay for not holding his head steady.

I don't know why I'm staying on the

team, thought Boots sourly. *All he does is chew me out.*

The only satisfaction Boots got out of it was that Coach Dekay chewed out all the other linemen, too. He didn't miss any of them.

"I've got some sad news for you guys," said Bo Higgins after practice was over.

"What is it?" asked Boots.

"No practice tomorrow."

"Sad? You call that sad? That's the best news I've heard this week!"

"Hooray!" shouted the guys.

"I love practice, though," confessed Bud on their way home. "I can play football every minute every hour every day."

"That's because you're quarterback," grunted Boots. "You wouldn't say that if you played tackle or guard."

"I think I would."

"I would, too," said Duck. "I played guard last year and I loved it. I loved to break through and hit the quarterback. It was a real challenge."

"Oh, yeah?" said Boots. "Then why aren't you playing on the line this year?"

"Because Coach Higgins asked me to play in the backfield. Heck, I'd play any position he wants me to."

Boots didn't know whether Duck was giving him a line of baloney or what.

The game with the Flyers started at one-thirty sharp. The Flyers won the toss and elected to receive. Leo Conway kicked off and a Flyer caught the ball on the twenty and carried it up the field to the thirty-two.

Mark Sawyer, the Flyers' left tackle,

played opposite Boots. He was a couple of inches shorter than Boots but big around the chest and shoulders. Every time the ball snapped, Mark rammed his helmeted head into Boots. The Flyers picked up two first downs on runs at Boots's side before the Apollo tackle got wise to Mark.

The next time the ball was snapped Boots side-stepped Mark, pushed him aside and plunged through the wide gap after the quarterback, Ray Shaff. He saw Ray hand off the ball to a halfback running toward his right side of the line. Boots knew he'd never be able to get the ball carrier, but he might be able to throw a block on one of the Flyers. He raced after a backfield man who was attempting to throw a block on an Apollo guard, reached him and flung himself against the guy's

legs. The man went down like a bale of hay.

The whistle shrilled as the ball carrier was tackled on the Apollos' thirty-eight-yard line. A flag was down and Boots saw the referee pointing a finger at him.

"Clipping!" cried the ref.

Boots was stunned.

"You hit the man from behind, kid," explained the ref. "That's illegal and a fifteen-yard penalty."

The ball carrier had gained six yards on the run, so the Flyers chose to accept the penalty, which gave them nine more yards and another first down.

Two more plays and the Flyers scored a touchdown. A short pass into the end zone gave them a 7 to 0 lead.

I knew I should've stayed home, thought Boots unhappily.

6

JACKIE PRESTON ran the Flyers' kickoff back to the Apollos' thirty-one. The Apollos moved forward in running plays and the quarter ended with the Apollos in possession of the ball.

Third down, three to go, and the ball was on the Apollos' forty-six-yard line.

"Eighteen," said Bud Davis in the huddle. "Don't forget to button-hook in, Pete."

"Right," said Pete.

Eighteen was a pass play from Bud to Pete with the line back-pedaling to screen Bud.

47

The men broke out of the huddle and went into their positions.

"Down!" barked Bud. "Fourteen! Twenty-two! Eight! Hut! Hut! Hut!"

Bud took the snap from center and faded back, the linemen back-pedaling to screen him, then chucked a short pass over the Flyer center's head. Pete Ellis caught it on the run and barged to the Flyers' forty-one for a first down.

"Eighteen flare," said Bud in the huddle.

Eighteen flare was a pass to the right end behind the line of scrimmage. The team scrambled into position.

"Down! Forty-six! Sixteen! Eight! Hut! Hut! Hut!"

Bud took the snap, faded back . . . back. Boots had control of his man for a few moments, then suddenly stumbled

48

and the Flyer tackle swept past him. Boots was just in time to block the middle linebacker. By then Bud had thrown the ball in a beautiful spiral pass to the right side of the field to Pete Ellis. Pete snared the pass and galloped for a touchdown, his man never farther than a yard behind him.

The guys whooped and hollered, and the Apollo fans cheered and whistled.

"Nice pass, Bud!" a fan shouted.

"Great run, Pete!" yelled another.

See who gets the credit? thought Boots. The quarterback and the end. Nobody thinks about the linemen. Bet no one except Mom and Dad and Gail knows that I'm out here.

Leo kicked for the extra point. The kick was good and the score was tied.

Tony Alo went in with five minutes to go before the half. "Nice work, Boots!"

someone yelled from the stands as Boots came running to the sideline.

Someone wants to be nice, thought Boots. Some people are even clapping. Maybe they're clapping for Tony.

Boots removed his mouthpiece, scooped up a dipperful of water, rinsed his mouth, then brushed a towel across his hot, sweaty face. With one minute left to go Leo kicked a field goal from the eleven-yard line to put the Apollos ahead, 10 to 7.

The boys sucked on slices of oranges during the fifteen-minute rest period, and Boots wished he had a sandwich too. He was famished.

Coach Higgins had him start the second half. This time the Flyers kicked off. Duck Farrell caught the ball on his side of the field, pulled away from two would-be tacklers by some tricky broken-field running, got good blocking from Richie Powell and Ralph Patone, and was downed on the forty-eight.

In two plays they carried the ball to the Flyers' eighteen.

"Let's get it over," said Bud. "Eighteen."

The play was a pass to right end Pete Ellis.

It failed badly. The pass was intercepted in the end zone and the Flyer safety man raced down the left side of the field and all the way for a touchdown. A pass into the end zone made it 14 to 10.

Boots saw Bud shaking his head and kicking the grass at his feet. He's certainly sick over that, thought Boots. I would be, too, I suppose.

The teams lined up for the kickoff. It was an onside kick that barely traveled the necessary ten yards. The entire Flyers team rushed for the ball, but Duck landed on it and smothered it with his body.

The Apollos tried a line buck and an end-around run, netting them six yards. A flag was dropped on the next play and the referee rolled his hands, indicating the offside penalty, then pointed at the Apollos.

"C'mon, Boots! Watch it!" cried Bud.

Boots's face turned crimson. He had taken a step forward and gotten back in time, but his opponent had jumped forward and made contact with him before the ball was snapped, making Boots responsible for the five-yard penalty.

The next play fooled the Flyers completely. Bud faked a handoff to Leo, who charged through right tackle as if he really had the ball. Boots's job was to brush his opponent to the right, then throw a block on the middle linebacker. He did.

Meanwhile, Bud faded back and then heaved a long bomb down the right side of the field to Pete Ellis. Pete was alone. He caught the ball and raced to the end zone. The kick for the extra point was off to the right. No good. Flyers 14, Apollos 16.

The Flyers threatened twice to score in the final quarter when they had the ball within ten yards of the Apollos' goal line. But both times the Apollos held. As Boots wrote to Tom that night:

We won the game in the third quarter on a long pass to Pete Ellis. Bud's a pretty good quarterback. He's wise at times, just like a lot of the other guys. I try not to pay any attention to them, though. There's no use getting sore over things like that.

I did lousy, as usual. The ref called a clipping charge on me and an offside penalty. Heck, I hardly moved on the offside. The kid opposite me jumped and made contact. I think he did it on purpose so we would be penalized.

I'd better go to bed now. Neither Mom nor Dad knows that I'm writing this letter. I'm writing it in my room and it's getting late. So long.

Love,
Boots

7

PRACTICE went as usual the following week. Each day Boots promised himself that he wouldn't go to practice. He was sick and tired of being hit, pushed, and knocked around. He was through.

But by late afternoon of each day a certain feeling would return. Something would urge him to go.

He threw blocks and banged his head and shoulders against either Tony Alo or the other tackle who played in Tony's place. And he'd get blocked and feel head and shoulders banging into him, too. Now and then he'd let his opponent sweep past him after the ball carrier, not caring because it was only practice, not a real game. Or he'd let the opponent knock him on his fanny and he'd just lie there, waiting for the whistle.

He got chewed out but good from Coach Higgins.

"What's the matter, Boots? Are you tired already? We've just started. I've told you and the other guys that when the season started, if you don't want to play football, hand in your uniform. There are other kids who want to play."

It was surprising how those few words affected him. He didn't like to be yelled at. None of the kids did. He thought about it while lying in bed. And he realized that he couldn't blame the coaches. If he was a coach he'd get mad too if his players put only half of their effort into practice. They might perform the same way in a game.

He realized, too, that being yelled at didn't hurt him one bit. It always did him good. He played better. That was why he was in there playing. If he didn't put all his effort into the game the coach would have someone else in his place.

A letter arrived from Tom on Friday. It was addressed to Boots.

Dear Boots,

Your letter came this morning and you can't know how happy I was to receive it. You'd be surprised how many guys here hope for mail and don't get it. Mail can make a day for a guy. Sometimes a whole week if he gets it from somebody special.

You asked for my opinion if it's okay for you to tell Coach Higgins you don't want to play anymore. Okay, here it is. DON'T. You'd be sorry later.

I'm really glad to hear you're playing on the line. Playing guard and tackle are two tough, responsible positions. It's the line that makes a team what it really is.

What good is a quarterback if his offensive line is so weak that the opponents can go through it like water through a sieve?

Good luck to the Apollos. And let me hear from you again.

Love,

Tom

The Apollo-Starbird game was played on the school field. The day was cool and cloudy.

The Starbirds kicked off. Bud Davis caught the end-over-end boot near the right sideline and carried it back to the Apollos' twenty-eight.

Boots crouched at the scrimmage line, facing his opponent, Nick Sarino, eye to eye. Nick was built like a barrel. When

Boots heard the snap call he bumped into Nick and it was like jamming his shoulders against a cement wall. Nick grunted and pushed like a young bull and Boots felt himself giving ground. The whistle ended the scuffle.

"We gained about four," said Bud in the huddle. "Let's try twenty-eight. Pete, make sure you block your man."

"Don't I always?" replied Pete.

Boots heard the snap call and put a block on Nick that kept the big boy under control until Duck Farrell had time to take the handoff from Bud and race to the right side of the line. The play netted eight yards and a first down.

A run to the opposite side of the line picked up three yards. Then Bud unleashed a long bomb to left end Eddie Baker which Eddie caught and carried to the Starbirds' fourteen before the safety man pulled him down.

A line buck resulted in a four-yard loss. A short pass to right flanker Jackie Preston got the ball back to where it was, and another pass to Pete in the end zone did the trick. 6 to 0. Leo Conway's kick was good. 7 to 0.

The Starbirds' left safety man caught Leo's kickoff on the twenty-four and started up the field in a twisting, dodging run that first eluded Ralph Patone, then Vic Walker, then Boots. Boots had a hand on him but the kid slipped away as if he were greased. Blockers stopped Eddie, Leo and Duck.

Suddenly only Bud Davis was between the ball carrier and the goal, and the ball carrier was fast. Too fast for Bud. He went all the way.

The pass for extra point was good and the score was tied, 7 to 7.

"How do you like that?" grunted Richie. "A seventy-six-yard runback for a touchdown. I'm sick."

"I had my mitt on him," Boots fumed, "and he slipped away."

In the second quarter Bud fumbled Ralph's snap and Boots's man, Nick Sarino, fell on the ball. He hit it so hard Boots thought that the big boy would drive it into the ground.

In three plays the Starbirds moved the ball to the Apollos' three-yard line. They tried to buck the line twice but failed. With the ball on the one-yard line, Jerry Malley, the Starbirds' quarterback, shot a quick pass to his left end. Pete Ellis knocked it down.

Fourth down.

"Hold 'em, you guys!" yelled Bud. "Hold 'em!"

Yeah, hold 'em, thought Boots. *Buck your head. Bang your shoulders. Take the bruising. And who cares?*

Then he remembered Tom's letter and a change swept over him. He crouched with one hand on the ground, the elbow of his other on his knee. He looked at Nick determinedly.

Jack Malley took the snap, handed off to his fullback, Charlie Haring. Charlie lowered his head and drove toward a narrow gap on Boots Raymond's side of the line. Boots bumped Nick hard in an effort to knock the big boy aside and stop Charlie.

Instead, he slipped to one knee and

Nick stumbled past him. Disgusted, Boots didn't move. An instant later he saw Charlie rushing past him and through the hole he had left unprotected. Then he moved. But it was too late.

8

THE STARBIRDS threw a pass and it clicked for the extra point, making the score 14 to 7.

Tony Alo came in and jerked a thumb at Boots. "Out," he said. Boots stared at him, then ran toward the sideline.

"You gave up out there," said Coach Bo Higgins as Boots came trotting in. "You dropped to your knee and just stayed there. Don't tell me you got hurt because you sprang right up when you saw the ball carrier rush by you."

Boots flushed. He clamped his mouth shut and glued his eyes to the ground.

"Hurry off before we get penalized for having twelve men on the field!" snapped the coach.

Boots put on a burst of speed until he crossed the out-of-bounds line, then turned around with his back to the crowd. Somewhere in the stands were his mother, father and sister. They couldn't have heard Bo Higgins talking to him, though. Bo hadn't raised his voice that loudly.

The Starbirds kicked off. Bud caught the ball and ran it back to the Apollos' twenty-six.

Boots watched Tony Alo playing in his place, trying to drive Nick Sarino back. His mouth curved in a half smile as he saw Nick push Tony back like a feather.

Second and nine.

Bud faked a handoff to Leo, then pitched a lateral to Duck. Duck sped around left end and picked up five yards.

Third and four.

Again Bud faked a handoff to Leo. The fullback plunged through tackle as if he had the ball. Then Bud faded back, lifting his arm to pass. A Starbird sprang on him like a cat, tackling him before he could release the ball.

When the tackler rose Boots saw that it was Nick Sarino.

"A four-yard loss," grunted Bo Higgins. "That Starbird tackle went through as if nobody was there." He looked at Boots. "See how important your position is? A weak line is almost as bad as not having a line at all."

The statement sounded very much like the one in Tom's letter: "What good is a quarterback if his offensive line is so weak that the opponents go through it like water through a sieve?"

The Apollos went into punt formation. Leo Conway stood almost on his twenty-yard line, hands stretched forward, waiting for the snap from center. Bud barked signals and center Ralph Patone snapped the ball. Leo caught it and booted it before a Starbird end could get to him. The kick was high and short. It bounded near the fifty-yard line and was downed by a Starbird on the Apollos' forty-nine.

Jerry Malley handed off to his left halfback on the first play and the back sped around right end for a neat eight-yard gain. The Starbirds picked up a first down on a rush through tackle, then tried another run around left end. Leo Conway, playing the middle linebacker position, stopped him after a gain of four yards.

Charlie Haring then blasted through a hole in the Apollos' line that was wide enough to drive a truck through, and safety man Bud Davis downed him on the eight.

Boots saw Tony sprawled on the ground, helpless after a cross-body block from Nick Sarino.

"Tony! Get on your feet!" yelled the coach. He looked at Boots. "What's the matter with you guys? That ground so soft you'd like to go to sleep on it?"

Boots laughed. He couldn't help it. Sometimes Coach Higgins could be real serious and still utter a wisecrack funny enough to make you laugh.

The laugh was short though. Jerry Malley, the Starbird quarterback, faked a handoff to Charlie Haring and then shot a quick pass into the end zone to his right halfback. A kick between the uprights put the Starbirds even farther ahead, 21 to 7.

Cheers went up for Jerry for throwing a beautiful pass and to the halfback for catching it. You would think they were the only guys playing.

Even playing halfback or fullback would be okay, reflected Boots. I'd have a chance to carry the ball, then. I'd feel as if I'm really doing something. I don't have that feeling playing on the line. I'm just there to fill a space, get banged up and yelled at. Anybody can do the same thing.

He started the second half. He didn't care whether he did or not. The Starbirds had a pretty fat lead and the Apollos would need at least three touchdowns, or two touchdowns and a field goal, to beat them. But the Starbirds weren't just going to sit out there on the field, grooming their feathers. They'd want to score more touchdowns.

"Back again?" asked Nick Sarino as he faced Boots on the scrimmage line. "I thought you went home for lunch."

"Wish I had," grumbled Boots.

The Apollos had kicked off and it was the Starbirds' ball on their own thirty-two. First down and ten.

Charlie Haring took the handoff and started to plunge through the left side of his line. Nick bucked Boots with his head and shoulders, knocking Boots back a couple of feet. Boots saw Charlie bursting

through the hole Nick had opened up for him. Mustering all the strength he could, Boots brushed Nick aside and tore after the oncoming fullback. He stopped Charlie cold directly on the line of scrimmage.

"Nice tackle, Boots!" praised Bud Davis.

Duck slapped him on the rear and laughed. "Yeah! Keep it up and you might become a tackle!"

Second and ten. Jerry tried a forward pass to his left end. Pete Ellis knocked it down. A second try succeeded for a five-yard gain. The Starbirds then punted. Leo caught the spiraling kick and carried it back to his forty-three.

The Apollos crossed midfield and went deep into Starbird territory, but couldn't score. The Starbirds took over the ball and were on the Apollos' thirty-one when the third quarter ended.

The teams changed goals and the Starbirds started off with a long pass by Jerry Malley to his right end. The pass clicked and the end ran to the eleven before he was pulled down.

"We've got to stop them," said Bud Davis in the huddle. "Shall we try a blitz?"

"Why not?" said Leo. "Maybe we can make them fumble."

"Okay. Leo and I will hang back in case Jerry passes. The rest of you bust through the line."

Oh, sure, thought Boots. *Just like that. I can see you've never played on the line, Bud, old boy.*

Boots looked at Nick eye to eye. At the snap he bucked Nick with his shoulder, then brushed past him and tore after the quarterback. Jerry was fading back, both hands on the ball, looking for a receiver.

74

Suddenly his right hand lifted to his shoulder. The hand came forward.

Boots's head struck Jerry. At the same time he wrapped his arms around Jerry's waist and pulled him to the ground.

He felt the hard thump as both of them hit the turf. A few seconds later he heard the blast of a whistle. When he lifted himself from Jerry he saw a red flag on the ground near him and the ref pointing an accusing finger at him.

"Unnecessary roughness, kid!"

Boots stared at him, then at Bud Davis standing in the end zone, holding the football. A sad, depressed look was on the safety man's face.

"What happened?" asked Boots perplexedly.

"Bud intercepted the pass," answered Duck Farrell grimly. "That's what happened. But you goofed it up by tackling Malley *after* he had thrown the ball."

"So the ball is still theirs," added Leo gloomily. "Except that it's a lot closer to our goal than it was before."

9

THE STARBIRDS accepted the penalty. Naturally. The ref spotted the ball half the distance to the goal line. Since it was originally on the eleven, this put the ball on the five-and-a-half-yard line.

In a quick huddle Bud said, "Blitz 'em again! Just watch it this time, will you, Boots?"

Boots nodded.

The blitz didn't work. Jerry handed off to Charlie Haring, who broke around left end for the Starbirds' fourth touchdown.

They failed to score the point after, but they didn't need it.

The Apollos carried the kickoff to their own thirty-nine and moved the pigskin like a machine across midfield to the Starbirds' nineteen. Bud unleashed a long bomb that sailed in a beautiful arc directly into Pete Ellis's waiting hands, and the little end went over for a touchdown.

Leo's kick was good. But there were only two minutes left to play and they weren't enough. The Starbirds won, 27 to 14.

"Well, Boots, old boy," said Duck as they started off the field. "I guess you're not so hot on the football field, are you?" He was carrying his helmet under his right arm. His hair was like a wet, matted rug.

Boots yanked off his helmet and

brushed back his sweat-drenched hair. "I never said I was."

Duck chuckled. "No, but you wish you could be."

The remark stung and Boots glared at Duck. "Thanks a lot."

"Sorry. I shouldn't have said that."

"That's okay."

They walked along in silence for a while, Boots mulling over Duck's remark: *No, but you wish you could be.* He might as well have said that I want to show off, thought Boots.

He had heard Dad talk about "grandstand players," athletes who try to impress the crowd. Is that what Duck thought he'd like to do? If so, a lot of the other players on the team probably did, too.

Just because he preferred to play quarterback rather than any other position. Just because playing quarterback would put him in the middle of plays all the time.

He was no show-off, no matter what Duck or anybody else said. If he seemed to appear that way, he didn't mean it. Thinking back, he realized that he must have seemed to appear that way quite a lot.

"See you later," said Duck, and ran across the street in the direction of his home.

"Yeah," said Boots. He saw several people standing on the next corner. Mom, Dad, Gail and the Davises, Bud's parents, were waiting for him.

"Tough game to lose, wasn't it?" said Dad as Boots reached them and they started to walk homeward.

"Yes," said Boots glumly.

Mr. Davis smiled. He was tall, even taller than Dad, with prematurely white hair.

"You played a good game, Boots," Mrs. Davis said excitedly. "I think you boys would've won if the game had lasted a little longer."

Mr. Davis chuckled. "That's the way it usually is for the loser, isn't it, Boots?"

Boots forced a grin. "I guess so," he said.

"Do you like playing tackle?" asked Mr. Davis.

Boots shrugged. "I'm not crazy about it," he replied honestly.

"Pretty tough, isn't it?"

"Yes. But I suppose they're all tough."

"Do you know which position Bud thinks is the toughest, Boots?" inquired Mrs. Davis.

He grinned. "Quarterback, I suppose."

"No. Tackle! A lot of running plays are through tackle, he says. So whether you're on the offensive or defensive you have to work harder than any other member on the team."

Boots listened, surprised. "Well, I don't know about that," he said. "Bud works pretty hard, too. Calling the right signals isn't easy."

Bud was a broadminded kid. He'd think of things like that.

After supper Boots read Tom's letter again. Reading it was almost like having Tom in the room with him, talking to him.

I'm really glad to hear you're playing on the line. Playing guard and tackle are two tough, responsible positions. It's the line that makes a team what it really is.

You can say that again, brother, thought

Boots. Look how the other guys and I played on the line today. It's a wonder we weren't beaten worse than we were.

Good luck to the Apollos. And let me hear from you again. Love, Tom.

Boots folded the letter and put it back into the envelope. He sure missed his brother. How long had he been gone? Two months? Three? It was closer to four, he realized.

He returned downstairs and found Mom and Dad in the TV room, watching a show. Gail, her bare feet cocked up on a hassock, was nibbling on a cracker and reading a book. He couldn't understand how she could concentrate on reading with the TV blatting away.

He remembered what Mrs. Davis said about Bud after the game today and thought about calling him up and asking him to come over and watch television with him. Bud had never been here. They weren't such close friends that he could pick up the phone and say, "Hey, Bud, this is Boots. Come on over."

He dropped the thought.

After school on Monday the Apollos had scrimmage practice. Boots played defense. He burst through the line like a small truck and tackled Leo, Jackie, Duck — whoever took the handoff from Bud. Twice he broke from blockers and hit Bud before he could make a play.

Pete Ellis, coming from right end, took a handoff from Bud on an end-around play but never made it to the scrimmage line. Boots pulled him down for a five-yard loss.

"Playing good ball, Boots!" cried Coach

Dekay elatedly. "Why don't you play like that in a game?"

Boots pretended he didn't hear. But the remark made him feel pretty good.

10

DEAR TOM,
    I had a lot of fun at football practice today. The coach put me on offense and defense and I busted through the line and tackled whoever carried the ball without any trouble. Mr. Dekay, the assistant coach, said that I played good and wondered why I don't play like that in a game. I'll see what I can do this Saturday against the Argonauts.

Thanks for your letter, Tom. And for telling me not to give up. You sure made me see things about the tackle position I had not seen before. I was thinking about quitting, but I don't think I will now. I think I'll stick it out.

We're all praying for you and hope that you'll be coming home soon. I wish you were here now. Gail is okay, but I think it's more fun to have a brother in the house. There are some things you can't talk about with a sister. Like sports. She likes football, but she would rather talk about clothes. Or the latest book.

Well, take care of yourself. Mom and Dad are fine. We all send you our love.

Boots

He took the letter downstairs and left it on the hutch.

"You can read it if you want to," he said. "I haven't sealed it yet."

"We received a letter from Tom today," said Mom. "Did you see it?"

He frowned. "No."

"It's on my desk," she said. He got it and read it:

Dear Mom, Dad, Gail and Boots,
    I used to think I'd want to travel all over the

world, but, believe me, once I get home I'm going to stay there. Of course, being here in Vietnam isn't the kind of traveling I had in mind. We see a lot of sights. Some are interesting, some aren't. I think you know what I mean. But there isn't the freedom here I would want as a traveler. Well, we're here on business. We're not tourists.

Don't worry about my eating. We always have a lot of chow.

In fact, don't worry about me at all. I'm okay. I just miss you. Is it my fault that you're the greatest family a guy could be blessed with?

Write soon. All of you. And you, too, Boots. I'm anxious to hear about the Apollos.

Love,

Tom

He refolded the letter. "You think he's homesick, Mom?"

She smiled and shrugged. "What boy in his situation isn't? I'm glad you answered his letter, son. Gail or I — one of us writes to him almost every day. He'd get a kick out of hearing more often from you, too."

"Yeah. I guess he would. Well —" He glanced from his mother to his dad sitting across the room, reading a paper. "I've got homework to do. Then I'm going to sack out. Good night."

"Good night, son." They said it almost together.

He finished his homework in half an hour and went to bed. Man, he was bushed. That scrimmage practice had taken more out of him than any had ever done before.

His performance in the drills on Tuesday was almost as good as it was on Monday. Then it gradually changed. On

Wednesday it wasn't quite as good and on Thursday it was worse.

"What's happened, Boots?" asked Coach Dekay. "You lose your gumption somewhere during the week?"

Boots shrugged. He didn't know what to say.

"You had a lot of spirit and enthusiasm on Monday," Coach Higgins chipped in. "Each day since then Coach Dekay and I noticed that you were slacking off. You feel okay?"

"Yes. I feel fine."

But he didn't. He realized now that he was feeling the same as he had felt in the beginning, when he had gone out for football and the coach had put him at the tackle position.

Why play a position he didn't like? A

position he didn't fit into? Wasn't that like trying to put a round peg into a square hole?

Maybe it was just luck that he did so well in practice on Monday, he thought. He would never be a good tackle. Never.

11

BOOTS STARTED in the game against the Argonauts, who had won a game and tied one. Lynn Giles was their quarterback, a lefty who could throw as far as any kid Boots had ever seen. They looked sharp in their bright orange uniforms and were bigger, man for man, than the Apollos.

The Apollos won the toss and Bud Davis chose to receive. Jackie Preston caught fullback Smokey Mills's long kick and carried it back to the Apollos' forty-two-yard line. Duck burrowed the left side of the

93

line for a three-yard gain, then took a handoff from Bud and went around right end for two more yards.

Boots Raymond kept his man from plunging through both times, but he wished he were in Duck's place on those runs. He was the ball carrier. He and Bud and Leo and Jackie. Next in order of importance were the receivers, ends Pete and Eddie.

The rest of us are like the bottom men of a totem pole, thought Boots. All we do is to try to keep the enemy from busting through when we're on offense, and try to break through and bring down the ball carrier on defense. We're the workhorses.

In the huddle Bud called for seventeen flare, a pass play to Eddie behind the line of scrimmage. Boots felt more like going for a bicycle ride than playing football.

"Down! Seven! Four! Twenty-one! Hut! Hut! Hut!"

One moment the Argonaut tackle was looking directly into Boots's eyes, the next he was sweeping past Boots so fast that Boots didn't know what had happened. He turned and saw that the tackle had knocked down Bud's pass.

Bud glared at him. "What were you doing, Boots? Taking a nap?"

Boots walked reluctantly into the huddle.

"We've got to kick," said Bud. "Kick it a mile, Leo."

Leo Conway punted the ball close to the Argonauts' twenty-yard line. One of their safety men caught it and carried it back to their thirty-nine. Smokey Mills hit the line on Boots's side, but Boots knocked his man aside and stopped the fullback cold

95

before he could reach the line of scrimmage. A loss of two yards.

"Nice going, Boots," said Bud. He
chewed you out when you goofed, but
praised you when you did well.

Second and twelve. A halfback took a
handoff from Lynn and crashed through
the other side of the line for four yards.

On the next play Boots lunged forward
a fraction of a second before the ball was
snapped. The quarterback handed off to
the right halfback, who sprinted toward
his left side of the line. Boots flung his man
aside and bolted after the ball carrier. He
tackled him for a loss of three yards, but
when he got up he saw Duck pointing at
a red flag lying on the ground.

"Yeah," admitted Boots. "I know. I was
offside."

The Argonauts accepted the penalty.

The ref paced off five yards against the Apollos and spotted the ball on the Argonauts' forty-six.

Third and three.

They'll probably throw a short pass, thought Boots, to get a first down. He listened to the signals, then moved at the snap. He bumped his man aside then stood there, waiting to calculate Lynn Giles's move. But Lynn was fading back . . . back. He was looking at a receiver down the field.

Boots dug his cleats into the ground and sprinted forward, realizing now that he was too late to stop the quarterback.

Lynn threw. The pass was a long spiraling bomb that hit his receiver perfectly near the left sideline. The man raced the remaining twenty some yards for a touchdown. Smokey Mills kicked for the extra point and it was good. 7 to 0.

The Argonauts kicked off and once again Jackie Preston caught the ball and ran it back, driving almost to midfield before he was tackled. The Apollos moved the ball into Argonaut territory and got it to the twelve when again the Apollos were penalized five yards for being offside. This time Neil Dekay, the left guard, was the offender.

"Watch it, Neil," pleaded Bud. "Let's not goof things up now."

Second and fifteen. Bud called for a pass play. Boots, concentrating on the tackle opposite him, never saw the Argonaut linebacker come tearing through the line past him. He hit Bud. The ball squirted from Bud's hands. The Argonaut scooped it up and raced down the field to the Apollos' forty-three before Bud, himself, pulled him down.

"Boots! Richie!" cried Bud. "That guy busted through as if nobody was on the line at all!"

"Sorry, Bud," said Richie. "My man blocked me but good."

Boots said nothing. His eyes met Bud's and he knew that Bud was expecting him to mutter an excuse, too. But Boots looked away and headed toward his position at the line of scrimmage. Just then the horn blew, announcing the end of the first quarter, and the teams exchanged goals.

The game resumed, and Boots realized that something was missing. He couldn't get excited about the game. He just crouched there on the scrimmage line because it was a job he had to do. He looked

100

his man eye to eye and listened for the snap call. At the call he tried to brush his man aside and go after the quarterback, but he found himself pushed back to the ground.

He felt the same way during the next play and the next. He just couldn't get going, and he didn't care. The Argonauts moved down to the four-yard line without giving up the ball, and every now and then Boots heard Bud yelling to the guys — "Tighten up the line!" and "Block your man!"

Tony Alo rushed onto the field and patted Boots on the shoulder. "Take off, Boots," he said.

Boots trotted off the field.

"Come on, Boots! Move!" rasped Coach Bo Higgins's harsh voice.

He ran hard until he crossed the sideline, then stopped, took off his helmet, and sat beside a sub on the bench.

A shadow crossed in front of him and he recognized the coach's pants and shoes. "You all right, Boots?" asked the coach.

Boots didn't raise his eyes higher than the coach's knees. "I'm okay," he said softly.

"Look at me, Boots."

Boots looked up. Coach Higgins's eyes were mild but curious. "Are you telling me the truth, Boots?"

"Yes, I am. I'm okay."

"Then something's on your mind. What is it?"

"Nothing."

"That didn't look like you out there during those last few plays. You looked like a kid who had never played ball before."

Boots flushed. "I don't have any excuse, Coach, except that —" He broke off.

"Except what?"

"I don't know. Sometimes I just can't get excited about playing. This must be one of the times."

"You know what that sounds like, Boots?" said the coach. "Like a fat excuse. You know you don't mean that and I know you don't mean it. Something else is bothering you and I'm going to let you sit on that bench till you get it out of your system."

It was almost at that very moment that Lynn Giles went over on a quarterback sneak. Then Smokey Mills kicked the extra point, putting the Argonauts even farther in front, 14 to 0.

12

THE ARGONAUTS kicked off. This time the ball sailed end over end to Duck Farrell in the left corner. He ran the ball back up the field, weaving and dodging would-be tacklers, and was downed on the thirty-eight.

Bud pulled off a pass play first thing, heaving a bomb to left end Eddie Baker. Eddie caught it past the fifty-yard line and ran it all the way. An Argonaut safety man was less than two yards behind him but never could catch him. Leo kicked the extra point and the score was Argonauts 14, Apollos 7.

The cheers of the Apollo fans rang out loud and clear, but the quarter went by with the score unchanged. Twice Tony Alo tore through the line and tackled an Argonaut ball carrier for losses of two yards and four yards each. Boots tried to ignore him, telling himself he didn't care how well Tony played. For all he cared Tony could play every minute of every game.

During halftime Duck asked him how he felt. He thought Boots was sick. Jackie, Leo and Eddie wondered, too. "I'm okay," he told them. "I'm fine."

Coach Higgins and Coach Dekay had the boys assemble with them just beyond the north goal. The coaches of the Argonauts had their boys assemble with them just past the south goal. Here we go, thought Boots. A talk from the coaches: *Now, listen, men! You played like a bunch of clowns that first half! I want you to go out that second half and blah, blah, blah* . . .

But it wasn't like that at all. All Coach Higgins said was, "You did fine, boys. They just played a little better than you did, that's all. You know how to play football. Do the best that's in you. That's all Coach Dekay and I ask."

Five minutes before the second half started both teams got on the field and did jumping exercises to limber up their arms and legs. At last the whistle blew to start the second half and Boots put on his helmet and snapped the button. He was ready to go.

"Hold it, Boots," said Coach Higgins. "Tony's starting at right tackle. The rest of the lineup remains the same."

Boots stared at him. He couldn't believe it. Sure, he hadn't felt like playing that first half. But he felt like playing now. He wanted to, now.

Duck was beside him. They looked at each other.

"I don't understand it, Duck," said Boots. "I've always started."

Duck smiled. "Maybe one of these days you'll find out that you just can't have your way all the time, Boots. You think that Coach doesn't know you're sore because you can't play in the backfield? Don't be a lunkhead. Just because you're a big kid and can knock any one of us on his can whenever you feel like it has made you think you're King Tut. Well, on the football field you're just Boots Raymond. You've got a job on the line, and whether you're good at it or not depends on you. Nobody else. And if you don't give it your best, Coach Higgins will give somebody else a chance to do it. And you know what? Tony Alo isn't doing bad at all. If I were you I'd watch out for him. He just might take over your position permanently."

By the time Duck got through talking, Boots's face was almost as red as a beet. A couple of times he wanted to tell Duck to shut up his big mouth, but he didn't. He knew Duck was right. Every word the guy said was just as true as day.

The third quarter went by with him watching it from the bench. Tony played pretty good ball. Now and then Smokey Mills or one of the Argonaut halfbacks zipped by him, but he made a few tackles and hustled every minute. He didn't have the weight that Boots did, though. Nor the speed.

He's got the fight, the spirit, thought Boots. And I don't.

The Argonauts scored again in the fourth, but failed to kick the extra point. 20 to 7. They kicked off to the Apollos and Bud ran it back to the Argonauts' forty-eight. His first signal call was for an end-around run by Jackie Preston. On the next play Jackie took the handoff from Bud, started toward left end, then handed off to Duck Farrell. The play momentarily fooled the Argonauts who were going after Jackie till they were almost upon him. By then Duck had crossed the scrimmage line and had picked up another first down before a safety man nailed him.

First and ten and the ball was on the Argonauts' twenty-six. Boots rose from the bench and looked at Coach Higgins. He hoped to catch the coach's eye, hoped that the coach would tell him to go in and send out Tony Alo even though Tony was playing excellent ball.

Leo Conway picked up three yards on a through-tackle run, and the two-minute warning signal was called. Two minutes, thought Boots. Maybe time enough to score a touchdown, but not time enough to win the ball game.

He got to thinking about his poor playing during the first half and could have kicked himself. If any one guy was to blame for losing the game it was he.

Leo plowed through the line for another gain, this time for four yards. Third and three. Again Leo plunged through right tackle. This time he was stopped cold. Fourth and three.

Bud passed. Pete Ellis caught it just beyond the scrimmage line and was downed almost instantly. But it was another first down and the Apollo fans shouted like crazy.

The seconds ticked off. One minute to go. The ball was on the Argonauts' fifteen-yard line. Leo crashed through left tackle for two yards, then Duck ran deep around left end and was tackled on the eight. Third and three.

Bud smashed through on a quarterback sneak and scored. Then Leo kicked the extra point. Argonauts 20, Apollos 14.

Thirty seconds to go. Leo kicked off. The Argonauts carried the ball back to their twenty-nine. They moved it across midfield when the whistle blew. It was over.

"I suppose you'd like to pound the heck out of me, wouldn't you?" said Duck as he and Boots started off the field.

Boots grinned. "Why? For what you said to me?"

"Yeah."

"Well, I don't. But you got guts telling me all that. Nobody else has. Except Bo Higgins and Mr. Dekay, but they might not say it the way you did."

"It isn't guts," said Duck.

Boots frowned. "Oh, no? What is it, then?"

"Being friends, that's what. I would never have said that to you if I didn't like you, Boots. You're a nut, but I like you."

"I like you, too, Duck. I must be nuts. But I do."

Mom and Dad and Gail received letters from Tom during the week. Both were short, hardly filling one page. Both were very much the same. "I'm thinking of you all the time," he wrote in Mom and Dad's letter. "When I get home I'm going to eat hotdogs and hamburgers and listen to my favorite records till both my stomach and eardrums burst. See you. Soon, I hope."

In Gail's letter he wrote: "Hi, Gail. How's my favorite girl? You know what I'm hungry for? Hotdogs and hamburgers. I'm going to stuff myself with them when I get home. And keep the needle of that hi-fi set red hot. I haven't heard good music since I left . . ."

"He's homesick," said Mom. "He doesn't say it but it's in every word he writes."

"All the boys over there are," said Dad. "Heck, it's natural."

Boots didn't think it was natural, though, when no letters came the next week. And none the week after that. Mom and Dad got worried. And so did he and Gail.

13

BOOTS TRIED not to think about what might have happened to Tom by reading over Tom's letters and doing the best he could in football practice.

What Duck had said to him that day stuck in his head, too. *On the football field you're just Boots Raymond. You've got a job on the line, and whether you're good at it or not depends on you.*

Well, he'd see to it that he'd be good at it. As good as he could be.

He hadn't started in the game against the Flyers on October 9. Tony Alo had.

After Tony had let a runner slip by him twice and made a couple of foolish moves — one was grabbing a face mask and the other was blocking a guy from behind, a clipping violation (and each cost a fifteen-yard penalty) — Coach Higgins had sent in Boots. That was during the middle of the second quarter. Boots played the rest of the game and the Apollos came off the field with a victory in their pockets.

He kept writing letters to Tom every other day. Mom and Dad and Gail kept up their regular pace, too. Sometimes Gail wrote a letter in the morning and another one before supper so that it would go out in the evening mail.

"Bet no one's getting as much mail as Tom is," said Boots one day.

"Let's hope so," said Dad. But he said it as if probably Tom weren't receiving any

mail at all. As if he weren't there to receive it.

Mom was pretty affected by not having
heard from Tom in a long time. She looked
worried and was silent most of the time.

It was cold on October 16, the day the
Apollos played the Starbirds. The Apollos
won the toss of the coin and chose to receive. Charlie Haring, the Starbirds' hefty
fullback, kicked off and Bud Davis caught
the ball and carried it back to his twenty-
nine.

"Thirty-two," said Bud in the huddle.
Thirty-two called for Leo to carry the ball
through the two hole.

They broke out of the huddle. "Down!"
yelled Bud. "Twenty-one! Twenty-eight!
Nineteen! Hut! Hut! Hut!"

The snap. Bud took it, turned and

handed off to Leo. The fullback charged through the line between center and right guard and was pulled down on the thirty-three. Boots, tangled up with the man he had blocked, untangled himself, bounded to his feet and trotted to the huddle, feeling light and peppy.

"Twenty-eight option," said Bud.

The play called for Duck Farrell to either run with the ball or pass to Pete Ellis.

Boots slapped Duck on the leg. "Surprise 'em, pal," he said.

Duck did. He took the handoff from Bud, started to run toward the eight hole at the far end of the line, then chucked a forward pass that looked like a soft balloon floating through the air. Pete jumped, caught it, pulled it into his arms and bolted down the field. He whisked past the safety man by a thread and galloped on for a touchdown. Leo's kick for the extra point missed.

Three and a half minutes later, after the Starbirds failed to keep the ball, Bud hurled a long spiraling pass to Eddie Baker. The little left end caught it on his thirty and ran to the Starbirds' two-yard line. Bud carried it over on a quarterback sneak for the Apollos' second touchdown. Again Leo's kick for the extra point failed. Apollos 12, Starbirds 0.

In the second quarter the Starbirds scored a touchdown on a twenty-yard pass from quarterback Jerry Malley to Charlie Haring. Charlie's kick for the extra point was good. Apollos 12, Starbirds 7.

The Starbirds kicked off. Bud caught the end-over-end boot and carried it to his twenty-six. In the first play he muffed the snap. A mad scramble for the ball followed, ending with the Starbirds in possession.

Bud looked sick. "My fault," he said.

"Let's get it back!" yelled Boots.

The Starbirds went into a huddle, broke out of it and the linemen hurried to the line of scrimmage. Boots looked Nick Sarino, his man, eye to eye.

"Forty-two! Thirty-eight! Seventeen! Hike!" barked Jerry Malley.

Boots shoved Nick aside and bolted through the line. He hit Jerry as the quarterback started to fade back. Jerry went down and the ball slipped from his hands. It bounced, Boots caught it, pulled it against his chest and started to run.

A halfback sprang at him. Boots stiff-armed him, dug his cleats hard into the turf and ran on. He crossed the fifty

. . . the forty-five . . . the forty . . . the thirty-five . . .

Finally — TOUCHDOWN!

Cheers exploded from the stands. Hands slapped Boots on the back. "Great play, Boots!" yelled Bud.

"Talk about surprises!" cried Duck, pumping his hand. "That one beats 'em all!"

The Apollos went on to win, 36 to 21.

That night Boots wrote a long letter to Tom.

Dear Tom,

We played the Starbirds this afternoon and gave them a real working over. We beat them 36 to 21 and can you believe it? I made a touchdown! I busted through the line and hit Jerry Malley, the quarterback. He dropped the ball and I picked it up and ran. It was something like a sixty-three-yard run. I never dreamed I'd ever make a touchdown, Tom. But I did.

You know, I owe almost everything to you for making me stick it out as a tackle. I really like it now. It's fun blasting through the line to get after the quarterback or whoever carries the ball. Guess who had the most tackles today? Well, I suppose you can guess after I asked you that silly question.

Anyway, your letters made me see a lot of things about playing tackle that I wouldn't have seen otherwise. Duck Farrell told me a few things, too, that put some sense into my head. I use to think he was a creep, like a lot of other guys. He's my best friend now. Next to him, I think, come Bud Davis, Leo Conway and Richie Powell. Heck, they're all pretty good guys once you get to know them.

We're playing the Argonauts next Saturday. It's our last game. So far we've lost two and won three. I'll let you know what happens.

Take care. And please write.

Love,
Boots

A week later Boots was leaving for the big game against the Argonauts when the phone rang. Gail ran to answer it. When she came back her face was flushed and her eyes white-rimmed as they darted from Dad to Mom.

"Who was it?" asked Dad.

"The post office," she said. "There's a special delivery letter for Mr. and Mrs. Thomas Raymond. The man wants to know whether you want to pick it up or have them deliver it on Monday."

Mom and Dad looked at each other. "Tell them I'll pick it up," Dad decided.

Boots tried to read the anxious look on Dad's face. Was that letter from Tom? Or was it about him?

He glanced at the clock on the kitchen wall. One o'clock. He had to go or he'd be late. "See you later," he said, and left.

The Argonauts were leading the league. They had won three games, lost one and tied one. The Apollos had to win today or finish in second place.

The Argonauts won the toss and chose to receive. Leo Conway's kick was a good one. Lynn Giles, the Argonauts' fast quarterback and safety man, caught the ball and carried it to their forty-two.

The Argonauts huddled, then broke out of it, and Boots found himself facing his opponent, Curly Hines. Lynn barked signals, the ball was snapped, and Curly threw himself to Boots's right side. Boots lost his balance, realizing instantly that Curly meant to open a hole there for the ball carrier. Boots saw Smokey Mills, the fullback, grab the handoff from Lynn and head for the hole.

Boots dug his cleats into the hard

ground and surged toward Smokey. His padded shoulders shoved Curly aside and he reached out as Smokey came forward. He hit Smokey and drove him back beyond the line of scrimmage. The whistle shrilled. Smokey tossed the ball to the ref, who spotted it at the point where Smokey had gone the farthest. A gain of a yard.

Boots grinned at Curly. "You're getting better, Curly. You almost knocked me for a loop."

"Oh, sure," grumbled Curly.

The next play was a rush through the other side of the line. Boots brushed by Curly and cut in front of the quarterback, his heels clawing up dirt as he swung his body to the left. He went after Smokey like a small tank and reached the fullback about the same time that Leo Conway, playing linebacker, did. The two brought

Smokey down, but the rugged Argonaut had gained three yards on the play.

Third and six. This time Lynn pulled a double reverse and it worked for a first down. Lynn kept the plays on the ground — no passes — and moved his team forward like a machine.

"C'mon, men!" shouted Bud exasperatingly. "Are we going to let them do this all day?"

The Argonauts reached the Apollos' thirty-two when they were finally stopped. Two running plays, one a try through Boots's side and the other an end-around, netted them a loss of two yards.

"Watch for a pass," Bud warned.

Bud's guess was right. Lynn faked a handoff to Smokey, then faded back and shot a bullet pass to his right halfback. The pass was good. The receiver carried it to the Apollos' eighteen where Bud Davis nailed him.

Smokey tried a run through right tackle — his right — and picked up four yards. On the second down the Argonaut center snapped a poor pass to Lynn. Lynn fumbled the ball. Boots saw it rolling loose and dived for it. At the same time he saw Curly diving for it, too. Boots fell on the ball first, covering it with his chest. Curly fell on top of him, followed by two other Argonauts, and Boots felt as though he were being buried. From a distance he heard the shrieking blast of the whistle. One by one the guys got off him.

He rose to his feet, feeling good all over.

"Nice going, Boots." Bud smiled and swatted him on his rear. "Now let's move it the other way."

14

THE BALL was spotted on the Apollos' nineteen. "Thirty-eight," said Bud in the huddle. "I'll fake a handoff to Jackie running left. Let's go."

The players broke from the huddle and formed at the line of scrimmage. "Down!" shouted Bud. "Twenty-four! Eighteen! Hut! Hut! Hut!"

The snap. Boots blocked Curly Hines and threw himself partly in front of a linebacker who came charging through the line. He stopped Curly cold, but the linebacker recovered his balance, backed away, and then tried to circle around him.

Boots got to his knees and threw himself in front of the man, a perfect block. A smile flickered on the tackle's face as he saw Duck throwing a block on the Argonaut end and Leo carrying the ball through the wide hole. The fullback raced twelve yards before the safety man pulled him down.

"Nice going, men!" cried Bud. "Boots! Duck! Beautiful blocking, you guys!"

First and ten. "Let's try it again," he said in the huddle. "They won't expect it."

Whether the Argonauts expected it or not the play worked like a charm, though for nine yards this time.

The Apollos picked up a first down and moved the ball to midfield when the horn blew, announcing the end of the first quarter. The teams exchanged goals. Bud's first call was thirty-eight again. This time the play worked perfectly. Duck blocked the Argonaut, giving Leo time to squirt through the wide hole, then the fleet-footed halfback raced ahead and blocked the safety man just enough to keep him from getting his hands on Leo, and Leo went all the way. He then kicked the extra point and the Apollos led, 7 to 0.

The Argonauts carried the kickoff back to their thirty-one and Lynn Giles's first play was a pass to his left end. The end went all the way to the Apollos' nine where Bud tackled him. Two plays later Lynn threw a pass into the end zone. Smokey caught it to put the Argonauts on the scoreboard. Smokey then kicked the extra point to tie it up. 7 to 7.

During halftime Boots thought about the special delivery letter. Was it from

Tom? If not, did it concern him? Boots looked for Mom, Dad and Gail in the stands, but the crowd was so thick he couldn't see them.

Two minutes after the third quarter started, Lynn Giles heaved another long spiraling pass to his left end. This time the end went all the way. Smokey kicked for the extra point. It wasn't good. Argonauts 13, Apollos 7.

Leo returned the kickoff to his twenty-eight. Just as he was hit the ball squirted out of his hands and an Argonaut recovered it.

"What's wrong with us?" exclaimed Bud. "We start off great, then all at once we fall apart."

"We've just got to play harder," said Boots. "These Argonauts are up to beat us. Do you see what their best play is?"

"Long passes," said Duck.

"Right. We stop those and we'll have them licked."

Bud nodded. "Jackie, stick closer to that left end. We have to double-team him. He's good."

The Argonauts' first play was an end-around run that got them nowhere. Smokey tried a line buck and got nowhere. Then Lynn faked a handoff to Smokey and faded back to pass. Boots brushed Curly aside, dodged past a linebacker and went after the quarterback. Lynn seemed to have trouble finding a receiver. He saw Boots charging after him. He tried to get away, but Boots grabbed his jersey, pulled, and then wrapped his arms around the quarterback and nailed him for a heavy loss.

Fourth and twenty-two. The Argonauts

went into a punt formation. Lynn waited for the snap from center while Smokey stood back in kicking position. The snap. Lynn got the ball. *Then he stood up and shot a quick pass to his left end!*

Suddenly a blue and white uniform swooped toward the ball. A pair of hands reached out and grabbed the pass. In the same motion the player started running in the opposite direction. He had an open field. He went all the way. Boots didn't know what had happened until he heard the fans shouting and saw Jackie Preston touching the football to the ground in the end zone.

Bud shot a quick forward pass for the extra point and it was Argonauts 13, Apollos 14.

In the fourth quarter Boots nailed Lynn again for an eight-yard loss. At another time he caused Lynn to fumble the ball which was recovered by Richie Powell, the right guard.

The Apollos moved ahead like a steamroller. And then Bud faked a handoff to Leo and Leo faded back and threw a long bomb to Duck that nailed the coffin on the Argonauts. Duck went over for the touchdown. Leo's kick missed, and the score stayed at 20 to 13, Apollos' favor. The Argonauts had the ball on the Apollos' twenty-six when the final whistle blew.

"We're champs!" yelled Duck, jumping around like a clown and throwing his helmet into the air.

Then they all threw their helmets into the air and started to jump and yell and whoop. Bo Higgins and Coach Dekay ran out to the field and praised the boys and then went over to shake hands with the losing coaches.

"Boots, you did great," said Bud Davis, a broad grin on his sweaty, dirty face.

Boots smiled. "Thanks, Bud. Guess we all did."

Someone grabbed his arm. "Boots!" cried Gail, her eyes wide as bottle caps. "Come on! We've heard from Tom!"

He stared at her. "You — you mean that letter?"

"Yes!"

He ran off the field, her hand still clinging to his arm. Mom and Dad were waiting at the sideline, smiling happily. Dad handed him the letter. "Read it," he said.

Boots's hand trembled as he held the letter and read:

Dear Mom, Dad, Gail and Boots,

I've been very busy these last couple of weeks, which is why you haven't heard from me. I was really in the thick of it. But I'm back now and I'm okay, so don't worry.

I used to get very lonely and discouraged. I don't know what I would have done if it hadn't been for your letters coming to me almost every day.

I am especially grateful to Boots for his letters. I think that we had our own private mutual determination society going between us. I told him to stick with football, and he did. And his letters have helped me to see my way through here, too — as much as yours did, Mom, Dad and Gail — because I think that both he and I have shared a common experience. Neither one of us enjoyed doing a job we were asked to do. But we did it because it was necessary.

The big difference is that one is a game, the other a war.

Take care, and don't stop writing.

Love,

Tom

138

A sense of relief filled Boots as he handed the letter back to his father.

"Well, we can relax now," said Dad, smiling. "Tom's okay."

Boots nodded. "I suppose that when he comes home he won't want to wrestle with me anymore," he said.

Dad chuckled. "Don't be too sure about that. You've come a long way, too, you know."

FINAL STANDINGS

	WON	LOST	TIED
Apollos	4	2	0
Argonauts	3	2	1
Starbirds	3	3	0
Flyers	0	5	1